THE ANT'S JOURNEY

ISBN 0-89868-531-1–Library Bound
ISBN 0-89868-532-X–Soft Bound
ISBN 0-89868-533-8-Trade

A PREDICTABLE READER

THE ANT'S JOURNEY

Story by Janie Spaht Gill, Ph.D.
Illustrations by Bob Reese

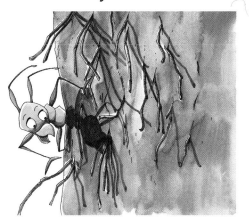

✳ ARO PUBLISHING

4

The ant left the anthill
to take a look around.

"Look!", he said, "a tall gray tree.
That's the first thing I found."

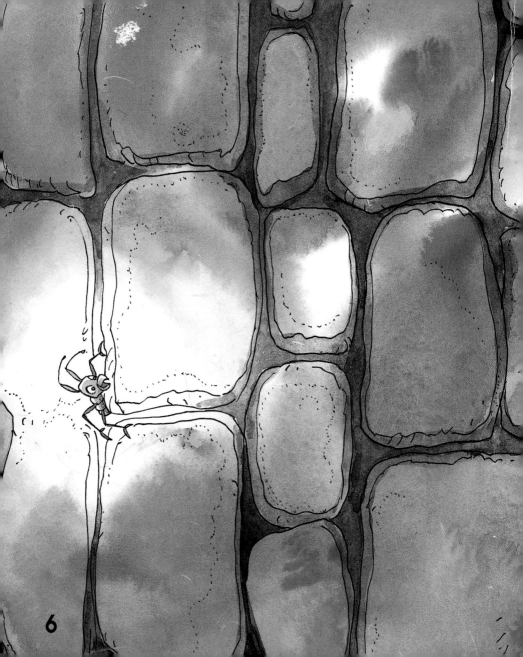

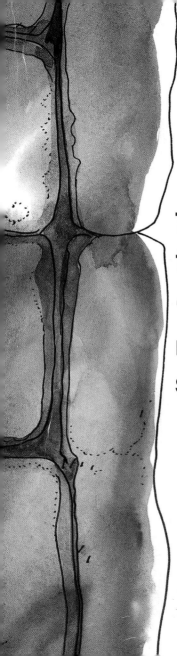

The ant left the tree
to take a look around.

"Look!", he said, "a great
red chimney. That's the
second thing I found."

8

The ant left the chimney to take a look around.

"Look!", he said, "a great blue ocean. That's the third thing I found."

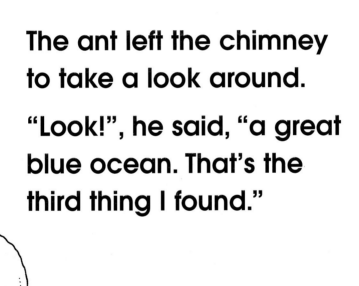

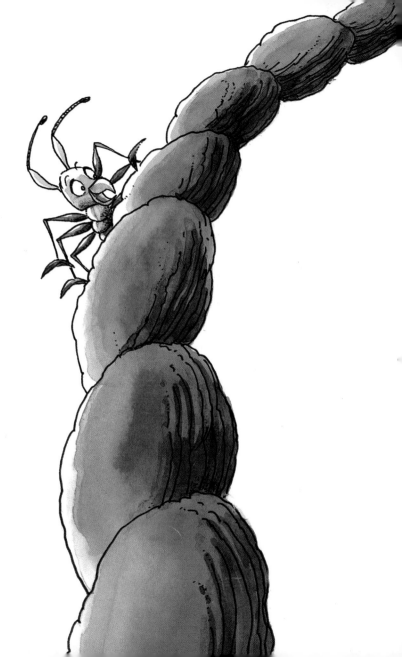

The ant left the ocean
to take a look around.

"Look!", he said, "a great
orange bridge. That's the
fourth thing I found."

The ant left the bridge
to take a look around.

"Look!", he said, "a great
white snow bank. That's
the fifth thing I found."

13

The ant left the snow bank
to take a look around.

"Look!", he said; "a great yellow moon. That's the sixth thing I found.

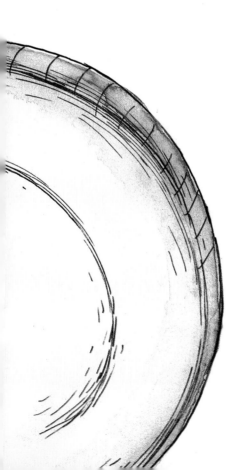

The ant left the moon
to take a look around.

"Look!", he said,"a great
brown log. That's the
seventh thing I found."

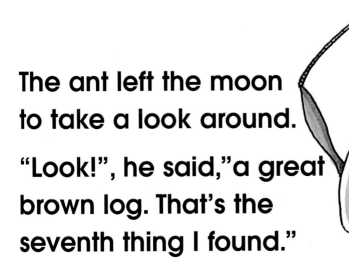

17

The ant left the log
to take a look around.

"Look!", he said, "a great
green mountain. That's
the eighth thing I found."

18

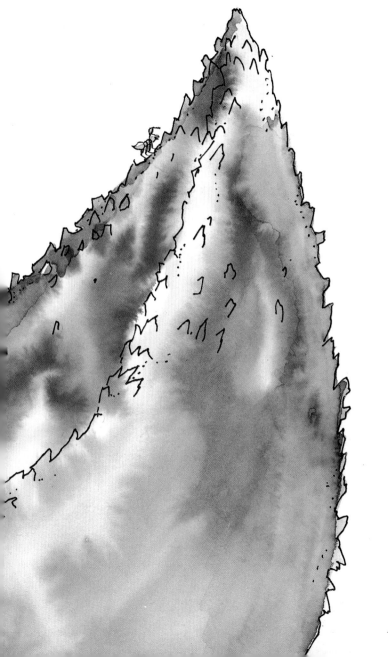

19

When the ant had reached
the end, he took a look around,
and this is what he saw, from
the top as he looked down.

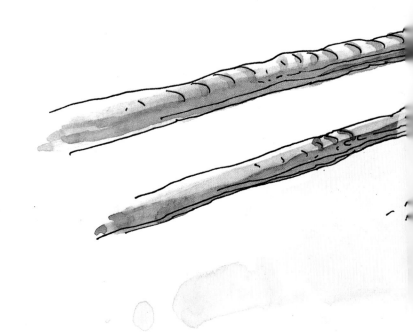

Now find the tree, the chimney, the ocean, the bridge, the snow bank, the moon, the log, and the mountain.